The Boxcar Children Mysteries

THE MYSTERY OF THE LOST MINE

THE GUIDE DOG MYSTERY

THE HURRICANE MYSTERY

THE PET SHOP MYSTERY

THE MYSTERY OF THE SECRET MESSAGE

THE FIREHOUSE MYSTERY

THE MYSTERY IN SAN FRANCISCO

THE NIAGARA FALLS MYSTERY

THE MYSTERY AT THE ALAMO

THE OUTER SPACE MYSTERY

THE SOCCER MYSTERY

THE MYSTERY IN THE OLD ATTIC

THE GROWLING BEAR MYSTERY

THE MYSTERY OF THE LAKE MONSTER

THE MYSTERY AT PEACOCK HALL

THE WINDY CITY MYSTERY

THE BLACK PEARL MYSTERY

THE CEREAL BOX MYSTERY

THE PANTHER MYSTERY

THE MYSTERY OF THE QUEEN'S JEWELS

THE STOLEN SWORD MYSTERY

THE BASKETBALL MYSTERY

THE MOVIE STAR MYSTERY

THE MYSTERY OF THE PIRATE'S MAP

THE GHOST TOWN MYSTERY

THE MYSTERY OF THE BLACK RAVEN

THE MYSTERY IN THE MALL

THE MYSTERY IN NEW YORK

THE GYMNASTICS MYSTERY

THE POISON FROG MYSTERY

THE MYSTERY OF THE EMPTY SAFE

THE HOME RUN MYSTERY

THE GREAT BICYCLE RACE MYSTERY

THE MYSTERY OF THE WILD PONIES

THE MYSTERY IN THE COMPUTER GAME

THE MYSTERY AT THE CROOKED HOUSE

THE HOCKEY MYSTERY

THE MYSTERY OF THE MIDNIGHT DOG

THE MYSTERY OF THE SCREECH OWL

THE SUMMER CAMP MYSTERY

THE COPYCAT MYSTERY

THE HAUNTED CLOCK TOWER MYSTERY

THE MYSTERY OF THE TIGER'S EYE

THE DISAPPEARING STAIRCASE MYSTERY

THE MYSTERY ON BLIZZARD MOUNTAIN

THE MYSTERY OF THE SPIDER'S CLUE

THE CANDY FACTORY MYSTERY

THE MYSTERY OF THE MUMMY'S CURSE

THE MYSTERY OF THE STAR RUBY

THE STUFFED BEAR MYSTERY

THE MYSTERY OF ALLIGATOR SWAMP

THE MYSTERY AT SKELETON POINT

THE TATTLETALE MYSTERY

THE COMIC BOOK MYSTERY

THE COMIC BOOK
MYSTERY

created by
GERTRUDE CHANDLER WARNER

Illustrated by Hodges Soileau

ALBERT WHITMAN & Company
Morton Grove, Illinois

ISBN 0-8075-5529-0

1 3 5 7 9 10 8 6 4 2

Printed in the U.S.A.

Contents

CHAPTER 1

The Missing Comic Book

Six-year-old Benny Alden put down the Captain Fantastic comic book with a satisfied sigh.

"That was cool," he said. "Especially when Captain Fantastic jumped over a building to catch the bad guys."

"It was a good story, wasn't it?" said ten-year-old Violet. They had read the comic together.

Jessie, who was twelve, glanced out the window of the boxcar.

"It's stopped raining," she said.

"Let's ride our bikes downtown and see if the new issue of Captain Fantastic is out yet," Henry suggested.

The boxcar was a great place to spend a rainy afternoon, but the Alden children were glad to be outside.

When their parents had died and they had no home, Benny, Jessie, Violet, and Henry had lived in the abandoned boxcar in the woods. But then Grandfather Alden found them and took them to his big house in Greenfield. Grandfather had the boxcar towed to the backyard so the kids could use it as a clubhouse.

Now the Boxcar Children rolled their bikes out of the garage and pedaled to the town square. They locked their bikes in the rack and walked into a small shop called Comic World.

"Hello," said a young man who was chewing gum. "What can I do for you?"

"Is the new Captain Fantastic here yet?" asked Benny.

"Just came in yesterday," replied the clerk, putting the comic on the counter.

As the oldest, fourteen-year-old Henry carried their pooled allowances. He paid for the comic and gave it to Benny.

"Need any back issues?" the young man inquired. "Comic World sells used comics as well as new ones."

"We have every issue except one," Jessie said. She kept their collection organized by issue number.

The clerk nodded. "I bet I know which one you're missing. Number nine, right?"

"How did you know?" asked Violet. She liked comics for the art. She was thinking about becoming an artist someday.

"There's a mistake in Captain Fantastic number nine," said the clerk, popping his gum. "You know that purple suit and green cape he always wears? Well, in the second story of number nine, the cape is *orange*."

The young man leaned on the counter. "The mistake makes it valuable. Collectors are hanging on to it. They don't bring it here to trade or sell."

"Will we ever find that comic?" Henry said. "We'd like to have a complete collection."

"It's not impossible to find number nine," the clerk answered. "There's an antiques show across town in the Greenfield Center. Some out-of-town comic book dealers are there. You might get lucky."

The Aldens thanked the clerk, then went outside. Henry said, "The Greenfield Center isn't far. Let's ride over."

The huge community building was packed with booths and dealers selling old furniture, paintings, lamps, rugs, coins, dishes, and books. Crowds of people escaping the rainy day clogged the aisles.

"Wow!" said Jessie. "It's like a bunch of little stores in one big store."

Violet spotted a display of old comics at a nearby booth.

"Let's try there," she said.

At that moment, a familiar figure turned away from the booth. He wore a purple suit with a green cape and a black eye-mask.

"Captain Fantastic!" Benny exclaimed. "He's real! No, wait. He walks too slowly and he doesn't have any muscles."

"It's a regular person dressed in a Captain Fantastic suit," Jessie told him.

Without saying a word, the masked man handed her a flyer, then strolled down the aisle.

"What does it say?" asked Benny.

"It says there's a meeting of the local Captain Fantastic Fan Club at the library this week," Jessie said. "And something about a big comic con next weekend in Hartford. What's a comic con?"

"I think it's short for convention," Henry said. "Comic book fans from all over the world will probably be there."

Ahead of them, the Captain Fantastic cruised the aisles, handing out flyers. He stopped briefly and spoke to a comic book dealer before hurrying off again.

"Do you have Captain Fantastic issue number nine?" Jessie asked the dealer.

The man shook his head. "The fellow in the cape asked me the same thing. That particular issue is as scarce as hens' teeth."

"I didn't know chickens have teeth," said Benny.

Jessie giggled. "They don't. It's an expression. It means the comic book is very hard to find."

The kids walked up and down each aisle, asking all the comic dealers if they had issue number nine. None did.

"Look, there's another comic booth," said Violet, pointing. "Over where that lady is standing."

The booth displaying racks of comics was half hidden in the corner. As the kids approached, a woman in jeans and boots was talking to the dealer intently.

"I wonder if she's asking for number nine, too," Jessie said. "So far we haven't had any luck."

The woman looked up at the kids, then back at the bald-headed man behind the stand. She tossed her reddish blond hair, spun on a booted heel, and stalked away.

"I don't suppose you have Captain Fantastic number nine," Henry asked without much hope.

"As a matter of fact, I do," the dealer replied. From beneath the counter, he pulled out a plastic bag containing the comic.

"Oh, boy!" cried Benny. They had actually found it!

"How much is it?" Jessie asked.

"Thirty dollars," the man replied. The plaque on his booth said his name was Al Conrad.

The kids stared at one another in disbelief. Thirty dollars for one comic book!

Henry was digging through his pockets. "Uh — we've only got twenty dollars — "

"You seem like nice kids," said Al generously. "I'll let you have it for twenty dollars. I like dealing with young fans."

Before Henry could count out the bills, the Captain Fantastic rushed up to the booth in a swirl of green cape.

"Number nine!" the costumed man exclaimed in a high-pitched voice. "Al, I must have it for my collection!"

"You're too late," Al told him. "I just sold my only copy to these young people. You should have gotten here earlier."

"I just now found your booth. I'll pay you

double," the Captain Fantastic offered, his voice rising even higher.

"Sorry," the dealer told him firmly. "I sold it to them and I can't go back on my word."

The Captain Fantastic left, his shoulders sagging with disappointment.

"I wish that guy could have found a copy, too," Benny said. "He must really love Captain Fantastic, to go around in a suit like his."

"Lots of fans wear costumes," Al said, slipping their purchase into a paper bag. "And this comic does turn up from time to time. I'm sure he'll find one eventually. Would you like to sign up for my mailing list?"

While Jessie filled out the Aldens' address, Al added, "He may find one at the comic con in Hartford this weekend. That's a much bigger show. You should go."

"I wish we could," said Violet wistfully. "But we just spent our allowances for the next two weeks."

"There's the refreshment stand," said

Henry, as they walked away. "We don't have any money, but we can get a drink of water."

Benny was so excited he didn't even mind missing a snack. "Can we look at our comic?"

At a small table, Violet removed the comic from its protective plastic bag. As she did, a slip of paper fell to the floor. She bent to pick it up.

"I guess this is our receipt," she said, then stared at the paper. "No, it's some kind of note."

"What does it say?" asked Jessie.

Violet turned the paper so they all could see. In strange lettering, the note read, *I'll try to get orig. of #9. "Sid."*

"What does it mean?" Jessie wondered.

"Maybe Mr. Conrad knows," said Violet. "Let's go back and ask him."

Al Conrad seemed surprised to see them back so soon.

"Do you know anybody named Sid?" asked Benny.

"Sid? Oh! That's the guy who writes and

draws Captain Fantastic," Al replied. "Sid Hoyt. See?" He pulled a new issue of the comic off a rack and opened it to the first page.

"I don't see any name," said Violet.

"The first page of a comic is called the 'splash' page," Al told them. "The top panel is always the biggest. Most artists sign their names somewhere in that panel. Sid Hoyt's signature box is always in the bottom left corner."

"It's very small," said Henry. "I've never noticed before."

"Mr. Hoyt is very modest," said Al. "Did you know he lives right here in Connecticut?"

"Really?" said Jessie. "Where?"

"I don't know exactly," Al replied. "Some little town. Why all the interest in Sid Hoyt?"

Violet pulled the note from the comic bag.

"We found this when we opened our comic."

Al glanced at the paper with a frown.

Then he laughed. "You think Sid Hoyt wrote this note?"

"We don't know," said Henry. "We don't even know what the note means. Do you?"

"It doesn't mean anything," Al said. "Just some foolishness left by the former owner, that's all. Now, if you'll excuse me, I need to pack up."

He stuffed the paper in his pocket and turned away.

"Excuse me," said Violet. "May we have the note back, please?"

Al hesitated, then handed it back to her.

The kids walked out of Greenfield Center and into the sunlight.

As they pulled their bikes from the rack, Benny commented, "Al seemed to be in a big hurry all of a sudden. Like he wanted to get rid of us."

"And why did he try to keep the note?" asked Henry.

"He said the note doesn't mean anything," said Jessie. "I think it means *some-thing*."

CHAPTER 2

A Surprise Invitation

"Do you have a green cape?" Benny asked Mrs. McGregor.

The housekeeper looked at Benny, who was wearing a purple T-shirt that belonged to Violet. The shirt came down to his knees.

"I'm afraid not," she told him. "But I have a green scarf. Will that do?"

With Mrs. McGregor's green silk scarf tied around his neck like a cape, Benny buzzed around the house. The Aldens' dog, Watch, scampered with him, barking at this new game.

When Benny was trying to jump over the footstool, he nearly ran into Grandfather.

"Whoa!" said Grandfather. "Who are you?"

"I'm Captain Fantastic!" Benny said.

"Oh, yes, the superhero character in the comic book," said James Alden. "Tell me, Captain Fantastic, what makes you so fantastic?"

"I can do anything!" Benny waved his arms for emphasis. "I can jump over buildings and run faster than the wind. I can swim like a fish and see in the dark."

"Well, Mr. Fantastic, it sounds like you'd be very handy to have around," Grandfather said, laughing.

"*Captain* Fantastic!" Benny protested. "Captain Fantastic does good all over the world. And when he isn't wearing his suit, he's an ordinary scientist. The kind that studies bugs."

"I smell something wonderful coming from the kitchen," said Grandfather. "I bet it's Mrs. McGregor's famous macaroni and cheese casserole. Maybe you ought to

change back into Benny Alden for supper."

Benny giggled. "It was me all along, Grandfather!" Then he ran upstairs to his room to change.

Violet, Jessie, and Henry were gathered around the window seat in the hall.

"Supper's almost ready," Benny told them.

"We were talking about the note we found in the comic," said Jessie.

"What about it?" asked Benny.

Violet patted the window seat cushion, inviting Benny to sit beside her. "We think it's important. Maybe it has something to do with the comic book artist Sid Hoyt."

"Like what?" Benny wanted to know.

"It's somehow connected to that issue number nine we bought," said Henry. "We'd like to find out more."

Benny's eyes widened. "Do you think we've found a mystery?"

"Maybe," said Jessie with a smile. It had been a while since the Aldens were last involved in a case. They were very good at solving mysteries. "Wouldn't it be neat if we could meet Mr. Hoyt? Maybe he would sign our special comic book."

"But we don't know where he lives," said Violet. "Al Conrad only said he lives in Connecticut. That's a whole state. He could be anywhere."

"How will we find him?" Benny asked.

"Let's ask Grandfather," Henry said. "He knows about things like that."

Grandfather did know how to find a person's address.

"Go to the Greenfield Library," he instructed them. "There are phone books for every county and major city in this state. If the person you're looking for is listed, he'll be in one of those phone books."

"We'll go tomorrow," said Jessie. *Maybe*, she thought, *we have stumbled onto another mystery!*

The next morning, the children rode their bicycles into town again. Along the way, they stopped to watch some construction workers building a new house. ANOTHER FINE HOUSE BY ROLLINS CONSTRUCTION, the sign proclaimed. Cars and trucks belonging to the workers were parked along the curb.

"They've done a lot more work on the house since last week," Henry commented. "Yesterday the crew was off."

Benny watched a worker sawing some boards. "I want to be a house builder when I grow up," he said admiringly.

"I thought you were going to be Captain Fantastic," said Jessie, teasing.

Then Benny noticed that the worker with the saw had long hair tucked up into her hard hat.

"Hey, that's a lady house builder!" he exclaimed.

"Don't be so surprised," said Violet. "Women can do any job they want, even build houses."

At that moment, the woman glanced up from her work and looked across the street at the Aldens as if she had heard them. Jessie knew the woman couldn't hear them over all the hammering. But something in the woman's intense stare made her nervous.

"We'd better get moving," she said, climbing back on her bike.

They pedaled swiftly to the library. Inside, Henry asked where they would find the Connecticut telephone books.

"Upstairs in the reference room," the librarian replied.

In the reference room, another librarian directed them to several phone books on a low shelf.

Henry pulled out all the phone books and put them on a table.

"Connecticut has eight counties," he said. "There is a phone book for each county, plus ones for the cities of Hartford, New Haven, and Stamford. I'll take four. Jessie, you take four, and Violet will take three."

"What will I do?" asked Benny. He could read a little, but not such tiny print.

"Find some paper," Jessie told him. She began skimming her first book. "Does 'Hoyt, S.' count?"

"Yes," said Henry, taking out the note they found in the comic book. "His name is Sid, but you might see 'Hoyt, Sidney,' too. Sid is usually short for Sidney."

The children were silent as they leafed through one book after the other.

Then Violet jumped up in excitement. "Bingo! I bet this is him!"

The others leaned in to read the entry.

" 'Hoyt, Sid, 145 Oak Tree Circle, Putnam,' " Violet read aloud.

Jessie nodded. "I found a 'Hoyt, S.' in this book, but your Sid sounds like he's the one." She carefully copied the information, including the man's phone number, on a piece of paper Benny found.

"Where is Putnam?" Violet wanted to know.

"I went to Putnam with Grandfather once," Henry said. "It's only about thirty minutes from Greenfield. What a lucky break for us!"

"Can we ride there on our bikes?" Benny asked.

Henry shook his head. "It's too far. Wait a minute."

He went over to the reference librarian

and came back with a folded pamphlet. "Here's a bus schedule. A bus goes from Greenfield to Putnam three times a day."

"We'll call Mr. Hoyt as soon as we get home," said Jessie excitedly. "If Mr. Hoyt says it's okay, I'm sure Grandfather will let us visit him."

Thump, thump, thumpity-thump!

Several books had suddenly dropped from the shelves of the bookcase behind the children.

"How did those books fall?" asked Violet.

"Let's check." Henry led the way around to the other side of the bookcase.

No one was there.

The children replaced the books on the shelf, then returned to their table.

The paper on which Jessie had written Sid Hoyt's address was still there. But the note they had found in the comic book was missing.

"The note is gone!" exclaimed Violet.

Jessie looked at Henry. "Are you thinking what I'm thinking?"

"That someone knocked those books out

so we would leave the table?" he said. "Yes, I think that's possible."

"Who took our note?" Benny asked. "And why?"

They looked around for clues.

Violet got down on her hands and knees. "Look at this." She brushed some yellowish powder near the table leg.

"That might be a clue," said Jessie. "But lots of people come in the library, so the powder may not have been left by the person who took the note. At least we have Mr. Hoyt's address and phone number. Let's go home and call him."

The Aldens rode straight home, not even stopping to see the progress on the new house.

They ran upstairs to use the phone in the hall.

"Who wants to call?" said Violet. "Not me!" She was shy and sometimes had trouble talking to strangers.

"I'll do it!" Benny offered.

"I'm sure Mr. Hoyt would love to talk to you, Benny, but maybe I should call him the first time," said Henry.

Jessie gave him the paper with the information.

Henry dialed the number, then waited. "I got his answering machine," he told the others. Henry left a message with the Aldens' phone number and the reason he called.

"Now we have to wait for him to call back," Benny said.

They didn't have to wait long. A short while later, Grandfather came out to the boxcar, where the kids were playing.

Benny jumped up. "Did Mr. Hoyt call us back?" he asked.

"No, but *Mrs.* Hoyt did." Grandfather grinned. "Nancy Hoyt is an old friend of Mrs. McGregor. They sometimes play bridge together. She invited you over to meet her husband — and they'd like you to stay for lunch!"

CHAPTER 3

The Barn in the Woods

The next morning the Alden children caught the first bus to Putnam. Thirty minutes later, they climbed off in Putnam's bus station.

Henry had brought a map. After consulting it, he said, "Oak Tree Circle isn't too far from here. We can walk."

It had rained the night before, but the day was freshly washed and pleasant. As the children walked away from the center of town, the houses became farther apart, with stretches of fields and woods in between.

"Here it is," said Jessie, pointing to a green street sign.

Violet felt a tingle of excitement. "I can't believe we're having lunch with a real cartoonist!"

The kids used a stepping-stone path to Mr. Hoyt's house. The house had a red roof and double front doors with iron hinges.

Benny stared. "What kind of a house is that? It looks more like a barn to me."

"Maybe it *was* a barn that Mr. Hoyt turned into a house," said Henry. "Some people do that."

The kids approached the front door as a big man rounded the corner.

"You must be the Aldens," he said in a hearty voice. "I'm Sid Hoyt. You may call me Sid. Did you have any trouble finding the place?"

"Not a bit," said Henry. "I'm Henry, and this is Jessie, Violet, and that's Benny. He's your biggest fan."

Sid laughed as he opened the door.

"Please, come in," he said, opening the door wide.

As Jessie entered the foyer, she studied their host.

Sid Hoyt had thinning gray hair and blue eyes. Although he was tall and broad-shouldered, his movements were gentle. He reminded Jessie of a big teddy bear.

She looked around. The bottom floor was one huge room that contained a sitting area with a granite fireplace, kitchen, dining area, and the artist's studio. A wrought-iron spiral staircase led to a sleeping loft. Floor-to-ceiling windows revealed a backyard with a well-kept garden and several large trees. Skylights brightened the workspace, which was on the far side of the living area.

A plump, gray-haired woman stepped forward to greet them. "You must be the Aldens," she said. "I'm Nancy, Sid's wife."

"I like your house," said Benny. "It's kind of like the boxcar we used to live in."

Sid raised his thick eyebrows. "You once lived in a boxcar? I'd like to hear that story over lunch. First, meet Batman and Robin."

Two sleepy cats uncurled themselves from a leather reclining chair. The large black cat yawned, while the smaller gray tabby blinked yellow eyes.

"You named your cats after superheroes!" said Benny, delighted.

"The black one is Batman," said Sid. "The tabby is his sidekick, Robin."

Benny bent to scratch Batman under his chin. "Can we get a cat?"

"We already have a dog," Jessie reminded him. "Watch might be jealous if we got a cat."

"Let me show you around," Sid offered.

"You have a lot of windows," Violet observed.

"Artists need lots of light," said Nancy. "And I like the way I can see my garden and the trees."

"It feels like the woods are inside," Violet said appreciatively.

They walked over to the studio area.

"This is where I work," Sid told them. "Sometimes the rest of the house might get messy, but I always keep my studio tidy."

An enormous slanted drawing table stood by the window, with hooded metal lamps clamped to the edge. Racks of bottled inks hung on one wall. Stoneware jugs held brushes, pens, and pencils.

"Wow! I never knew an artist would need so many cabinets," said Benny.

Sid pulled open a drawer of a metal filing cabinet. Inside were folders of pictures cut from magazines, photographs, and drawings.

"These are my picture files," he explained. "Artists need to look at objects when they draw them. Most of us aren't able to draw just from our imaginations. If I am drawing a car, for instance, it helps to refer to a picture of a car to make sure I have the details right."

"What is this?" Jessie pointed to a large white box with a glass cover.

"That's a light table." Sid turned a switch and the frosted glass top glowed. "It's used for tracing." He put a drawing on the glass and laid a sheet of blank paper on top. "See how the drawing shows through? Now you can trace it."

Henry noticed all the crayon pictures and

clay models of Captain Fantastic on the file cabinets.

"Who did these?" he asked.

"Fans," said Sid. "Kids send me drawings and comics they have made. Sometimes they build models of Captain Fantastic. Some are quite good."

Benny stood on tiptoe to get a better view of some penciled drawings taped to a drawing board.

"A new Captain Fantastic story!" he said, awestruck.

"Yes, that's the very latest issue," said Sid, smiling. "I'm putting the finishing touches on the black and white drawings so I can deliver it to my publisher tomorrow. There, other people will ink the drawings, add color, and letter in the words I've written."

"We just got a sneak peek," said Henry. "Before anyone else!"

Sid grinned. "You are definitely Captain Fantastic fans. Since you've come all the way from Greenfield, you must be hungry."

"I know you'll enjoy Sid's excellent cooking," said Nancy. "Unfortunately, I have an appointment in town, so I can't stay to eat with you. But it's always a pleasure to meet Sid's fans." She said good-bye to each of them, kissed her husband on the cheek, and hurried out the door.

The table was already set with cheery red, white, and blue place mats, blue stoneware dishes, and a vase of zinnias. Red glasses threw ruby rays of sunlight.

The children sat down as Sid came in with a tray holding a large bowl of chicken salad, warm blueberry muffins, and a platter of carrot sticks with yogurt dip.

Benny giggled as Batman stood on his hind legs and reached a black furry paw toward his plate.

"You have dreadful manners," the artist scolded the big cat. He put the cats outdoors, then returned to the table.

"Now tell me about your boxcar," Sid said.

Henry related the story of how they had found the abandoned boxcar in the woods and lived in it until their grandfather found them.

"Grandfather had our boxcar moved to his house," Henry concluded. "We use it as a clubhouse now."

"We keep our Captain Fantastic collection there," Violet added. "We have every single issue now. Even number nine. It took us a long time to find that one."

"We brought it with us," Jessie said. "If it's not too much trouble, we'd really like you to autograph it."

While the children were talking, Sid had been doodling his superhero character on paper napkins.

"A souvenir," he said, passing one to each of them. "And it will be a pleasure to sign your comic."

"I'll go get it." Benny ran into the living room where Jessie had left her backpack and raced back to the table with the comic in its plastic bag.

Sid carefully removed the comic from the bag. Then he leafed through the issue.

He put the comic on the table and looked at them with a frown.

"I can't sign this," he said flatly.

CHAPTER 4

The Secret Signature

"But why?" asked Benny, shocked. Sid had been so nice, giving them lunch and everything. Why would he refuse to sign their comic book?

"Because," stated Sid Hoyt, "your comic is a fake. I didn't draw it."

Jessie gasped. "A fake! Are you sure?"

"Positive. Wait here a moment." Sid went over to his studio and opened a cabinet. He took out a comic and came back to the dining table.

"This is one of the original printed copies

33

of issue number nine," he said. "In every is-sue I create, I hide a secret signature in ad-dition to the one on the splash page. It's just a fun thing I do. The signature is hidden on page two in this comic. Can you find it?"

The kids gathered around, trying to spot the signature.

Violet shook her head. "I don't see it."

"I'll give you a hint." Sid pointed to the third panel. "It's hidden in the fold of Cap-tain Fantastic's cape in that panel. Now can you find it?"

Henry spied it immediately. "There! Those lines in the folds of the cape by his knee are really your name. But it's really hard to see."

"Many fans know about my hidden sig-nature," Sid said. "But they haven't been able to figure out where it is. I always hide it in Captain Fantastic's cape. And I put it in a different place in each issue."

Jessie was comparing Sid's copy of num-ber nine with theirs. "Ours doesn't have the secret signature! Just lines."

"I'm afraid the comic you bought is

counterfeit," Sid told them sadly.

"Who made the fake comic?" asked Violet. "And why?"

"I don't know who is making the fakes," Sid replied. "But let me explain what happened with the original number nine. After I make my final pencil drawings, I write down what the colors are supposed to be. Kind of like a paint-by-numbers chart. Then I take the comic to the publisher. A person there, called a colorist, colors in the original drawings, using my notes."

"Did that person make the mistake on number nine?" Benny guessed.

"Yes, but only because I wrote the wrong color on the chart," Sid replied. "Instead of putting the number for green on Captain Fantastic's suit in the second story, I accidentally wrote the number for orange. The colorist didn't catch the slip, so number nine was printed with Captain Fantastic wearing an orange cape."

"I still don't see why that makes the comic so hard to find," Jessie said.

"Collectors think the mistake makes the

comic a curiosity," said Sid. "They either hang on to their copies or sell them at high prices. The comic is becoming scarce. I believe someone thought they could make a lot of money if they printed a fake version of number nine."

"We paid twenty dollars for ours," said Henry.

"I'm sorry," said Sid. "Where did you buy it?"

The kids told him about Al Conrad's booth at the antiques show. They also told him about the note that was stolen at the library.

"What did it say?" asked Sid, interested.

Violet replied, "It said, 'I'll try to get orig. of number nine. Sid.' Your name had quotation marks around it."

There was something else about the note that was strange, but she couldn't remember. They hadn't had the note long before it was stolen.

"Maybe 'orig.' is short for 'original,'" said Jessie. "And the quotation marks must mean it was someone *pretending* to be you."

"Like when you see a sign at a restaurant that says 'homemade cooking,' " Violet explained. "The quotation marks mean the food is *like* homemade cooking, but really it's cooked at a restaurant."

"The person who wrote the note must be the counterfeit artist," Henry concluded.

"Counterfeiting is wrong," Sid said sternly. "If other fans bought the phony number nine, they were cheated, just like you. I don't know who made the fake comic, but I want to catch him."

The Aldens looked at one another.

"This is your lucky day!" Benny said.

"How so?" Sid asked.

"We're detectives!" replied Benny. "We'll find the fake comic book artist for you!"

Sid smiled. "This *is* my lucky day! You're hired."

The children shook his hand to seal the deal.

"You bought the comic from a dealer named Al Conrad," said Sid. "Maybe he is part of the counterfeiting scheme. I've been to lots of conventions, but I've never heard of Al Conrad."

"There's a big comic book convention this Friday in Hartford," Henry remarked. "I bet he'll be there."

"I bet so, too," said Sid. "I'm going to the convention to give a talk about my work. I'm also auctioning off a piece of original Captain Fantastic art for charity. I really want this case solved. If my young fans find out they own a fake comic, they might think I'm behind the scam."

"Maybe only one fake comic was made," Violet suggested.

Sid shook his head. "Not very likely. It's expensive to produce a comic book and only print one or two copies."

"Do you think Al Conrad is involved?" Henry asked.

"I suppose he could be, but there's no way to tell right now," said Sid. "Besides," he added, "all of us in the comic book world — artists, dealers, fans — try to get along as much as possible. I can't very well point the finger at Al if I don't have evidence."

Finishing his lunch, Sid changed the subject. "I'm delivering the new issue of Captain Fantastic to my publisher tomorrow. Would you like to see it?"

"Oh, boy!" Benny said eagerly. "Would we!"

Sid Hoyt showed them the final illustrations, including the last page still taped to his drawing table. Notes in the margins referred to colors.

"It looks like a neat story," Benny told Sid. "It'll be even better in color."

"The drawings are great," Violet said admiringly.

"Violet's an artist, too," said Henry.

"We'll have to chat sometime," Sid said to her. "I'd like to know what kind of art you like to do best."

Violet blushed. A real artist was interested in her work!

Sid unzipped a big leather case and slipped the drawings inside plastic pockets on either side of the case.

"Why don't you come with me to the

publishing house tomorrow when I deliver the new comic. I'll give you a tour of the place."

"Would you really?" breathed Benny.

"You live in Greenfield. It's on the way to ABC Comics," said Sid. "I'll pick you up."

"I'll write down our address," Jessie said, fishing for paper in her purse. "You don't know how much this means to us. It's just — "

"Fantastic!" Benny finished for her.

Everyone laughed.

Henry checked his watch. "We'd better be leaving if we're going to catch the afternoon bus back to Greenfield."

"Would you like me to give you a lift to the bus station?" Sid offered. "It's no trouble."

"No, thanks," Henry said. "We have plenty of time and we enjoy walking. Thanks again for everything."

"I'll be at your house tomorrow at ten," Sid said.

"We'll be ready," Violet told him.

The children said good-bye, then left

Sid's house. The cats, Batman and Robin, were napping under an azalea bush in the garden.

"Isn't he a nice man?" Violet said. "I liked his wife, too."

"I hope we can help catch the comic book counterfeiter," said Henry.

Jessie, who was walking behind the others, kept glancing over her shoulder. The trees grew close to the sidewalk. Their long branches reached out like giants' arms.

She shivered, even though it was warm outside.

Violet noticed. "What is it?"

"I feel like we're being watched," Jessie said nervously.

"Do you see anybody?" asked Benny, looking around.

Jessie shook her head. "Not with all these trees — "

A loud *boom* interrupted her. The children jumped.

"It's just a car backfiring," Henry reassured them. "Probably that old clunker there."

A beat-up blue station wagon drove slowly along the road, causing traffic to back up. A white pickup passed the station wagon with a roar of impatience.

Benny watched the white pickup go by. He paid attention to cars. Where had he seen that white pickup before?

"Whew!" Jessie said, fanning her face. "One of those cars is blowing a lot of smoke."

"It must have a hole in its muffler," Henry said knowledgeably. "That's why it's so noisy. Hey, guys, we'd better hurry or we'll miss the bus."

They got to the bus station just in time. After settling into some seats across from each other, they discussed their new case.

"The note said the fake Sid is trying to get the original of number nine," Henry said. "Only, I'm not sure about the word *original*. Are the counterfeiters trying to find a real copy of number nine?"

Jessie shook her head. "I don't think so. The counterfeit artist has one already. He needed something to copy, after all, while he was drawing the fake comic book."

Violet spoke up. "Remember when Sid showed us the pieces of art he was going to bring to the comic book convention? He called it 'original art.' It was the very piece that he drew and painted himself, not just a copy of it."

"And that's why the counterfeiter wants it!" Jessie said suddenly.

"Wants what?" said Benny.

"The drawings that Sid showed us — the *originals*. They're the only evidence that the fake Sid copied the comic book and copied it wrong," said Jessie. "The secret signature is the proof."

"And if they get rid of the drawings, nobody will be able to prove that the counterfeiters did anything wrong," said Henry.

"When will the counterfeiter try to steal it from Sid?" Violet wondered.

"We'll have to stay on alert," said Jessie.

"We'll be ready for anything! Just like Captain Fantastic!" said Benny.

CHAPTER 5

Violet Remembers Something

"He's here!" Benny said excitedly, letting the curtain drop back from the living room window. He had been watching for Sid to arrive since breakfast.

"Benny," said Mrs. McGregor. "It's not polite to press your nose against the window." The housekeeper straightened the drape.

"I know, but I couldn't wait for Sid to get here," said Benny.

When the doorbell rang, Mrs. McGregor answered it.

"Nice to see you again, Sid," she said. "Please come in."

Grandfather and the children entered the living room to greet their guest.

James Alden introduced himself. "It's very nice of you to take my grandchildren to the publishing house today. They have talked of nothing else."

"I'm glad to have such enthusiastic fans," said Sid. He turned to the children. "Are we ready to go?"

"I've been ready for *hours*!" said Benny, grabbing his jacket and heading out the door first.

After everyone was buckled into Sid's dark green van, Sid pulled out of the driveway and onto the main road.

"How far is it to the comic book place?" Benny asked.

"About forty-five minutes," Sid replied.

"We were wondering how you became a comic book artist," Henry said.

"I used to doodle as a kid," said Sid. "I drew cartoons about a funny little character I made up. Then I put the cartoons in a

book. Other kids saw it and wanted copies."

The long drive passed quickly as Sid told the Aldens about how he kept drawing as a teenager and later went to art school.

"After art school, I got a job at ABC Comics, the comic book publishing house we're going to," he said. "I was hired as a 'cleanup' person."

"You mopped floors and took out the trash?" Benny asked.

Sid laughed. "The cleanup person erases stray lines. It makes the artist's job a little easier."

"How did you go from being a cleanup person to making your own comic?" asked Jessie.

"That's quite a story," Sid began. "I made a couple of friends at this place. One was the letterer and the other did the inking. You'll learn all about those jobs when we get to ABC Comics."

Sid told the Aldens that he and his two friends decided to create their own comic. They made up a superhero character and wrote and drew a sample comic book.

"But the idea was rejected," Sid said.

"You must have been really disappointed," said Violet.

"We were, but I didn't want to give up," Sid told them. "I created my own superhero, Captain Fantastic, and did another sample comic book by myself. This time, when I showed it to my boss, he bought it."

"Your friends must have been excited," said Henry.

Sid maneuvered the van onto another highway. "Actually, they weren't very happy, especially when Captain Fantastic was a hit. I was able to buy my house and work at home."

"Are you still friends with them?" Benny wanted to know.

Sid shook his head. "They both left ABC Comics. The letterer is now working for another comic book company. And the inker quit. I think she's doing something really different from art. I lost track of her."

"That's too bad," said Violet. "Friends should stay friends."

"I agree," said Sid, turning the van into a parking lot.

"Are we here?" asked Jessie. She looked at the one-story brick building in front of her.

Sid switched off the engine. "This is it. ABC Comics is a small operation. There are lots of little companies publishing comic books these days. Comics are popular, so it's a big business."

They got out and went into the building. Sid carried his leather case.

A pretty blond woman sitting behind the front desk greeted them with a smile.

"Sid! I'm so anxious to see the new comic!" she said.

Sid set his case on her desk. "I hope everyone likes it. Cindy, these are my friends Henry, Jessie, Violet, and Benny. They want to see how comics are made."

Cindy asked the children to sign the guest book. "Enjoy!" she said.

They began the tour.

"This is John," Sid said, introducing them to a young man sitting at a tilted drawing table. "He's the cleanup man here."

"That was your job once," Benny said.

John grinned at Benny. "I replaced Sid Hoyt when he left. He's famous now! Maybe one day I will be, too. As the cleanup person, I use this special eraser to erase smudges so the page is nice and clean."

Next they visited another young artist at a drawing table.

"This is Gus," Sid said. "He's the inker. Tell the kids what you do, Gus."

Leaning back in his chair, Gus explained that he inks over penciled drawings. Then he showed them his special pen and let them try it out on scrap paper.

In the back, the children met Lily, who was the colorist.

"You color in the comic," Henry said.

"That's right," Lily told them. "I use a key, or chart, that the artist has written out for me. Right now I'm painting the sky on this panel. It's supposed to look like night, so I'm using a dark blue watercolor."

On the walls, Lily had hung oil paintings of her dog.

"I like to do other kinds of art, too," she explained. "I'd like to paint people's pets for a living, but this job pays the bills."

The last stop was a desk in the corner. A young man named Chris stopped working to explain his job.

"I'm the letterer," he said. "I write the letters in the dialogue balloons."

"How did you learn to write like that?" Benny wondered.

"Practice," Chris said. "I learned from copybooks. Now I write like this all the time," he said with a laugh.

Violet studied the comic page he was lettering. Where had she seen that kind of writing before? Suddenly she remembered.

The note that fell out of their fake comic had been written in that style! The person who wrote the note was the one who made the fake comic, since it was signed "Sid." Could that person be a professional letterer, too?

Before Violet could mention this to the others, Sid took them around to see the rest of the company.

Benny had a question. "But where do you *make* the comics?"

"You mean, where are they printed?" Sid asked. "The publisher doesn't print comics. We send them to a printing company in another state and they print the copies. Will you all excuse me a moment? I have to let my boss know I'm dropping off the original art for the new Captain Fantastic."

The kids went back to the reception area. As they did, they saw Cindy zipping up Sid's leather case.

She flushed with embarrassment.

"I thought I saw a piece of paper sticking out," she said. "I didn't want it to get soiled." She hustled the case to a glass-windowed office in the back.

"I think she was peeking inside Sid's case," Jessie whispered.

"Maybe she's just nosy," Henry whispered back. "She said she was anxious to see Sid's new comic."

"Maybe she's a spy," Jessie said. "Sid said the counterfeiter needed help to print and sell the fake comic. Somebody who works in a comic publishing house. Why not this one?"

Just then Sid returned.

"How about lunch," he suggested. "Talking about comic books makes me hungry!"

"Me, too!" Benny agreed heartily.

Sid Hoyt took them to a little restaurant nearby. Framed drawings by comic book artists decorated the walls. The sandwiches and desserts were named after comic characters.

When their Captain Fantastic platters arrived, Sid asked the children if they'd had a chance to work on the mystery.

Violet told him about the lettering in the note. "It's just like the writing Chris uses."

Sid put down a french fry. "Most comic book artists can letter. But probably only a professional letterer, someone who writes that way so often that it becomes their normal handwriting, would use that style to jot a quick note. The counterfeiter may well be someone in the comic book business."

"There's something else," Jessie brought up. "We caught Cindy peeking in your case. She made up an excuse, but she acted guilty."

"Cindy *is* kind of nosy," Sid said.

Henry had been thinking. Everyone at ABC Comics acted as if they wished they had another job or were successful like Sid Hoyt.

"It's possible the person who made the fake number nine comic isn't a stranger," he said. "It could be someone you know."

"I've never thought of that," Sid said. "I just figured it's somebody out to make money."

Because it was late, they skipped dessert and headed home.

Benny, who was sitting in the backseat of the van, noticed a car behind them. It was a beat-up blue station wagon.

The station wagon followed them almost to the Aldens' house before turning off onto another street.

Was it the same station wagon they saw yesterday as they walked from Sid's house to the bus station?

If it *was*, their spy had returned.

CHAPTER 6

The Super-Aldens!

By the time Sid dropped the children off, dark clouds had gathered and it had begun to rain.

The kids dashed into the house and straight into the kitchen, laughing and shaking off raindrops.

Mrs. McGregor was waiting for them with a napkin-covered basket.

"I thought you might want a little snack," she said. "There's a thermos of milk and oatmeal-raisin cookies still warm from the oven in here."

"Oh, boy, thanks!" said Benny. "I'm starving!"

Jessie gave him a towel to dry his hair. "We just came back from lunch!"

"Yeah, but we didn't get dessert," Benny pointed out.

"Let's go out to the boxcar," Violet suggested. "I thought of something we can do."

Henry handed out umbrellas from the rack in the laundry room, then they ran across the backyard to the boxcar.

"What's your idea, Violet?" Jessie asked, setting Mrs. McGregor's basket on the table.

"Why don't we make our own comic book," Violet said. "Sid Hoyt drew comics when he was a kid. We can, too!"

"That's a great idea!" said Henry. "We can all work on it. Benny and I will make up the story."

"And Violet will draw the pictures because she's the artist," said Jessie, pouring the milk into mugs.

"You do the lettering," Violet said to her. "You have the neatest handwriting."

"What's it going to be about?" Henry asked, biting into a chewy cookie.

"Us!" Benny exclaimed. "We'll be superhero kids!" He jumped up from the table to "fly" around the room, nearly upsetting his milk.

"Benny, that's perfect!" Violet clapped her hands. "Our comic will be about four ordinary kids — "

"Who have special powers," Jessie said, picking up the story.

"The Super-Aldens each have a different special power," Henry said.

"And the Super-Aldens work together as a team to help save the world from evil," added Jessie.

Benny cleared the table so Violet could spread out their supplies: pencils, pens, markers, a ruler, and paper.

"What will our story be about?" Violet wondered, sharpening the pencils.

Henry thought a moment. "I think it should be our story. You know, how we found the boxcar in the woods. Only in-

stead of us staying ordinary, the boxcar gives us superpowers."

"Grandfather can look for us like he really did," added Jessie. "And he and all the people in Greenfield will hear about these superhero kids who fly and do neat things. But Grandfather won't know it's us until the end."

The children got busy. Henry and Benny wrote a story, with lots of help from Jessie. Violet drew the splash page. When she was finished, she passed it to Jessie, who wrote the dialogue in balloons coming from the characters' mouths. They all colored the pictures.

Two hours later, they had completed an eight-page comic book called *The Super-Aldens*.

"This is so cool," Benny said, flipping through the pages. "I wish we had more than one copy."

"That's a great idea," said Violet. "Let's make a couple and give one to Grandfather."

"The library has a color copy machine," Jessie said.

Henry checked his watch. "We'll have to wait until after dinner."

For once, the children ate in a hurry. Benny didn't even ask for second helpings. Grandfather excused them so they could ride their bikes to the library.

Benny rode ahead of the others, dodging puddles. "The workers are still at the new house. Can we watch them a few minutes?" he said, hoping the man with the bulldozer would shovel some dirt.

The Aldens braked their bikes.

Benny looked at the cars and trucks parked around the site. When he saw a white pickup truck and a blue station wagon, he remembered the spy.

"I forgot to tell you," he said to the others. "An old blue car like that one followed us today."

"Are you sure it was following us?" Henry asked.

Benny nodded. "I think it was the same car we saw when we left Mr. Hoyt's house."

"There are lots of old blue station wagons," Henry said. "But I'm writing down the license-plate number of this one just in case."

Jessie noticed the woman construction worker putting tools in a metal box. Today the woman wore overalls, with her braided hair tucked under her hard hat. Her boots were muddy.

"It feels good to rest a minute," Violet said, stretching. "We worked hard on our comic book."

"The pictures you drew are terrific," Jessie praised. "You could be a real comic book artist, Violet."

Violet polished her bike lamp with the hem of her shirt. "I'd love that," she said. "It would be hard work, but also fun."

"That lady is watching us," Benny said suddenly.

"The construction worker?" Henry looked across the road.

"Benny's right," Jessie said, lowering her voice. "She was putting tools away, but she stopped. I think she heard us talking."

Just then the woman turned and ducked into the new house.

"That was weird," Violet said. "She acts like we're bothering her."

"Maybe not," Henry said reasonably. "She could have forgotten one of her tools."

Or maybe, Jessie thought, *she didn't want us watching her anymore.*

The kids got back on their bikes and rode the rest of the way to the library.

Henry got change from the reference librarian, then led the others to the color copy machine in one corner. He fed the machine coins while Jessie made the copies.

Violet studied the bulletin board above the whirring machine.

"There's a good children's program coming up Saturday," she said. Just then another flyer caught her eye. "Hey! The Captain Fantastic Fan Club is meeting here tonight!"

"Can we go?" Benny pleaded.

"What time is the meeting?" asked Henry. They weren't allowed to ride their bikes on the streets too late.

"Seven," Violet replied. "It's five of now."

"We can stay an hour," Henry decided. "If it's okay with the people in the club."

Jessie finished copying the comic book, then asked what room the fan club was meeting in.

They found a lot of people inside the room, all chatting about Captain Fantastic and other comic books.

"I didn't know this many people liked comic books," said Benny.

A young man wearing a Captain Fantastic button squeezed by them, carrying a cooler.

"I wonder who he is," Jessie said. "I like his button."

The young man spoke over his shoulder to someone they couldn't see.

"Would you get the cups, Irene?" he said. "As soon as we set up the refreshments, we'll start."

Jessie realized she'd heard that voice before.

"We know that guy!" she said.

"We do?" Henry was puzzled. "I've never seen him before."

"Yes, we have," Jessie insisted. "We just didn't recognize him!"

CHAPTER 7

The Car in the Shadows

"Who is he?" Henry asked Jessie.

Benny noticed the way the man strolled, as if he had all the time in the world.

"He was the guy in the Captain Fantastic suit at the antiques show!" he said. "Remember, I said he was too slow to be Captain Fantastic?"

Violet nodded. "It *is* the same person. He was handing out flyers about this meeting."

Inside, fans traded and sold comics at a long table. Bottles of soda and a platter of store-bought cookies were on a smaller table.

The man wearing the Captain Fantastic button was arranging the paper plates and napkins, while a girl with straight black hair put out cups.

"I'm thirsty," said Benny. "Can we get something to drink?"

The kids walked over to the table. As Henry poured Benny a lemon-lime soda, the man stared at him.

"I know you," he said. "You're the lucky kids that found number nine at the antiques show."

"That's right," Violet replied. "Did you find another copy of the comic?"

He laughed bitterly. "Are you kidding? Number nines are really scarce. Change your mind about selling yours? I'll pay sixty dollars."

Henry shook his head. "No, thanks."

"You sure?" the man pressed. "How about sixty-five? Seventy?" He poured a cup of soda and gave it to Jessie. "Okay, seventy-five, but that's my final offer. You could buy a *lot* of comics for seventy-five dollars."

Jessie looked at Henry. They couldn't possibly sell their fake comic. That would be cheating this man, who would believe he was paying for the real thing.

"I'm sorry," she said. "But our comic isn't for sale."

The young man sighed. "Well, it was worth a shot. I'm Marvin Peabody, president of this Captain Fantastic Fan Club." He pointed to the dark-haired girl. "This is Irene. She's the club secretary."

Irene had short black hair and wore pink ballet shoes with her jeans.

She fixed drinks for Violet and Henry. "Are you interested in joining?"

"We really came by accident," Henry told her. "What time does the meeting end?"

"Usually by eight," Irene said.

"I've got to go start." Marvin turned back to the children. "I could go as high as eighty dollars for your comic."

"Sorry," Violet told him.

Marvin wheeled abruptly and headed for the front of the room.

The Aldens found chairs near the back and sat down.

"Is he mad because we won't sell him our comic?" Benny asked.

Henry gave a low whistle. "Eighty dollars is a lot of money! If he's willing to pay that much, I can't see why he hasn't found a copy. He's the president of the fan club."

Jessie nodded in agreement. "He must have had a chance to buy number nine before now. It seems like he really wants to buy *our* comic."

"All right, everybody! Welcome to our monthly meeting." Marvin shuffled through some papers. "Last month we began the contest to see who could find the secret signature Sid Hoyt hides in each of his comics."

The Alden children glanced at one another.

"The secret signature is the one clue the counterfeit comic book artist doesn't know about," Violet whispered. "Because it wasn't in the phony number nine."

Jessie nodded. "Let's hope nobody figures

out the secret signature is always hidden somewhere in Captain Fantastic's cape."

A thought occurred to her. *What if the counterfeiter is a member of this fan club? He could be in the room this minute!*

Irene raised her hand. "I think the signature might be on the last page of each issue. There's a funny little box in the lower left-hand corner. It doesn't really look like a signature, though."

"I know the little box you mean," said Marvin. "That's something the publisher puts in. Anybody else?"

Several people made guesses, but when everyone flipped through their Captain Fantastic comics, they realized each guess was wrong.

"We'll keep looking," said Marvin. "I talked to Mr. Hoyt about this some time ago. He just laughed and said it wouldn't be any fun if he told us where it was."

The meeting moved on to other business.

Henry turned toward Violet and pretended to wipe his forehead.

"That was close," he whispered to the

others. "Until we solve this case, Sid's secret signature must stay a secret."

"I have a surprise," Marvin was telling the audience. "Our club will have a private reception with Sid Hoyt at the convention this weekend!"

Cheers went up.

"As you know," Marvin continued, "Sid Hoyt is giving a presentation and will be auctioning off a piece of original art. And he will meet with us."

"Mr. Hoyt lives right in our area," said one of the members. "I wish he'd invite us to his studio sometime."

"We've been there," Benny blurted.

Everyone swiveled to stare at him.

"You've been to Sid Hoyt's house?" Marvin said in disbelief.

"Yeah," Benny said. "It's really cool. It looks like a barn."

"How did you get to see Mr. Hoyt's house?" Marvin demanded.

Henry spoke up. "We called him on the phone and he invited us."

"And then he took us to the place where

the Captain Fantastic comics are made," Benny added.

Marvin put his hands on his hips. "I've been president of this fan club for three years and he's never invited me to his home or to ABC Comics."

Irene laughed. "Oh, Marvin. Give the kids a break!"

The group discussed the upcoming convention a few more minutes, then Marvin ended the meeting.

As the Alden children were leaving the room, he caught up to them.

"I want to ask you guys something," Marvin said. "Have you known Sid Hoyt long?"

"We only met him this week," Jessie replied. "He's been really nice to us."

"I guess I have rotten luck, then," Marvin said with a tight smile.

"I'm sure that's not true," Violet reassured him. "Maybe we called him when he wasn't busy. He had just finished the newest Captain Fantastic comic."

"And he took you to ABC Comics to deliver it," Marvin said.

"We really need to go," Henry said, pushing the library's glass door. "We're not allowed to ride our bikes after dark."

In the parking lot, the members were getting into their cars.

As the kids unlocked their bikes from the rack, they saw Marvin come outside with Irene. Both carried boxes of leftover refreshments and paper goods.

"My comic book hobby is getting so expensive," Marvin said to her.

"At least you can buy what you want," Irene said, then walked across the parking lot to her car.

"Marvin's getting in that car," Jessie said, as they rolled their bikes onto the blacktop.

She nodded toward an old station wagon parked under a big oak tree. With the sun setting, the trees cast purplish shadows.

"It's too dark to see if it's blue or what the license plate says," Jessie said.

"Wait till he starts it," Henry said. "If it has a noisy muffler, we'll know it was Marvin who followed us from Sid's house the other day."

Marvin stowed the box and cooler in his trunk, then climbed into the driver's seat. But just after he closed the door, a motorcycle roared to life.

Both the motorcycle and the station wagon left at the same time. The kids couldn't hear if Marvin's car had a faulty muffler.

"We still don't know if Marvin is a suspect or not," Jessie said. "But we'd better head home or Grandfather will be worried."

As they pedaled out of the lot, Violet spied a small white card where Marvin's car had been parked.

"It's a business card," she said. "For Rollins Construction."

"That's the company that's building the new house," said Jessie. "I wonder if Marvin works for them."

"How come we've never seen him at the site?" Henry asked.

"We've seen a car like his there," Benny said. "I think it *is* Marvin's car. Maybe he hides when he sees us!"

CHAPTER 8

Scaredy Cats

Grandfather knocked on the open door of the boxcar. "You have a visitor," he announced.

Violet looked up from her drawing. "Hi, Grandfather. Who is it?"

Grandfather came inside, allowing Sid Hoyt to step into the boxcar behind him.

Sid Hoyt greeted the children and glanced around the room. "So this is the famous boxcar where you kids once lived. It's fixed up nice."

"The children drew a comic book," said

James Alden proudly. He held out the copy the kids had made at the library the night before. "I think it's quite good."

Sid paged through the comic. "It's *very* good," he praised. "I like the way you used the boxcar as the place where the Super-Aldens get their powers. You kids have great imaginations."

"Violet drew the pictures," said Henry.

"We're working on the second issue now," Jessie added.

Sid checked out the new panels on their table. "You kids may put me out of business!"

Everyone laughed.

"I came here for a reason," Sid told them. "I want to invite you to the comic book convention in Hartford on Saturday." He turned to Grandfather. "The invitation includes you, Mr. Alden."

"Oh, boy!" Benny shouted.

James Alden considered. "I have business in Hartford I've been putting off. Where is the convention?"

"Hartford Century Hotel," Sid replied.

Grandfather nodded. "I think that would work out fine. I'll drive to Hartford, and while you all are attending the convention, I'll take care of my business downtown. We'll stay at the hotel overnight and come back on Sunday. How does that sound?"

"Yay!" Benny cheered. "This is going to be fun!"

"I have another favor to ask," Sid said to Grandfather. "May I borrow your grandchildren this afternoon? You see, I am giving a presentation tomorrow. I have a lot of material to sort out and pack. My wife usually helps me, but she's working on a big project."

"We'd love to help," Jessie answered for them.

"I'll give them supper," Sid told Grandfather. "And bring them home before too late. We'll all need an early start tomorrow."

The kids climbed into Sid's green van parked out front and they drove off.

On the drive to Sid's house, they all discussed the mystery.

"We haven't found the counterfeiter yet," Henry admitted. "But some strange things have happened. Do you know Marvin Peabody?"

"The president of the Connecticut Captain Fantastic Fan Club?" Sid replied. "I know him. Why?"

"We saw him at the library last night," Jessie explained. "And he was at the antiques show where we bought issue number nine. He tried to buy it from us. When he saw us last night, he tried to buy the comic again. He offered us a lot of money."

"Not only that," Violet put in, "but he seemed kind of jealous that we're friends with you."

Sid sighed. "Marvin used to call me a lot and interrupt my work. I'm grateful for my fans. If nobody bought my comics, where would I be? But Marvin can be demanding."

"Why does he want to buy our comic so much?" Violet wondered.

"Good question," Sid said. "Marvin Peabody has a whole set of Captain Fantastic comics in mint condition. That means they are in Mylar bags and the covers have never been creased. I autographed a copy of his issue number nine at last year's Hartford convention."

Henry nodded. "It's like we suspected. Marvin just wants *our* number nine."

"But why?" Benny asked.

"Because he knows it's counterfeit?" Jessie guessed.

"Or," said Violet, "because he was supposed to get something from that particular comic."

"The note!" the others chimed in.

Sid pulled the van into the garage behind his barn-house. "I can see why you kids are detectives. You figure every angle."

As soon as Sid unlocked the door, Batman and Robin ran over, meowing. They weaved in and out of the children's legs, making the Aldens giggle.

"I think they're hungry," Benny said as Robin licked his fingers.

"Those two are always hungry," said Sid. "They'll just have to wait till suppertime."

Benny petted the cats. "I know how you feel," he told them. "I'm always hungry, too."

The Aldens followed Sid into the studio area. Sid opened the narrow, flat drawers of a long metal file cabinet.

"This is where I store my original art," he said. "I'm doing a presentation on issue number nine, since it's such a curiosity. People are interested in how I made the mistake on Captain Fantastic's costume."

Finding the right drawer, he pulled out several long sheets of white cardboard and laid them on the drawing table.

"Is that the original art for number nine?" asked Violet. The cardboard sheets were covered with tissue paper.

Sid handed one of the boards to her. "Raise the tissue — it's only hinged at the top."

Violet lifted the tissue cover, revealing bright drawings beneath of Captain Fantastic leaping across a river.

"I thought you did the drawings in pencil and wrote down the colors for the colorist at the comic book house," she remarked.

"You're right," Sid answered. "But I make full-color drawings for myself and for presentations. I also have the rough sketches, cover drawings, and the pencil finishes for each comic. They are all jumbled up, though. That's why I need your help."

The children sorted drawings and sketches for issue number nine. Sid chose the panels he wanted to use in his presentation. He set aside the splash page as the piece to auction off for charity.

"It should sell for a good price," he said.

They packed the art carefully in two portfolio cases, along with slides of the rest of the art that Sid would show using a projector.

"Do you keep the art for all your comics?" Henry asked the cartoonist.

Sid nodded. "ABC Comics sends the final pencil art back. My originals are probably the most valuable things I own. Art galleries frame these pieces and sell them."

"The counterfeiter wants the originals to

number nine," said Jessie. "Maybe he will try to steal the art at the convention."

"I've thought of that," Sid said. "I'm going to be really busy tomorrow. Will you help guard my art?"

The kids agreed.

Jessie thought, *I hope the counterfeiter does try to take the art. Then we can catch him!*

Sid heated some pork barbecue and the children set the table. While they ate supper, Batman and Robin gazed pleadingly at their plates.

"Shoo!" Sid said in mock anger. "You have cat food in your dishes."

Suddenly the cats scurried into the living room, eyes round with fear, tails fluffed twice their normal size.

"They don't act like that unless they are really spooked," Sid said, concerned.

Henry stared out the window. "They were looking this way. Somebody — or something — out there scared them."

Immediately everyone ran outside. They saw no one.

"Look at this!" Jessie called.

Under the dining area window, footprints marked the moist earth. A sprinkling of yellow powder edged one heel.

"That's the same stuff we found in the library when the note was stolen," Benny observed. He put some on his finger and sniffed. "It smells like the place where they are building the new house."

"Fresh-cut lumber," Henry agreed. "It's sawdust."

"So now we know the prowler and the person who stole our note are the same," Jessie concluded. "And that person works where wood is cut."

Violet placed her foot beside one of the prints. "Look how small these prints are. And not very deep. I think they were made by a woman."

"Or a small man," Sid added.

"Like Marvin Peabody," Henry said.

CHAPTER 9

Who Turned Out the Lights?

The sun was barely over the rooftops when the Aldens set out for Hartford. Mrs. McGregor sent them off with a goody bag filled with on-the-road snacks.

Two and a half hours later, Grandfather pulled their car into the entrance to the Century Hotel. The parking lot was packed. Vendors unloaded vans along the curb.

"Wow!" said Violet, peering out the window. "Look at all the people."

"This comic book convention is a pretty big deal," Henry said.

They all entered the plush lobby. At the busy front desk, Grandfather checked in and received room keys and a map of the convention floor.

They put their bags in their rooms, then Grandfather left for his meeting downtown.

The excited Alden children took the escalator to the second level, where the convention was being held.

Jessie gripped the handrail as they descended into a huge ballroom of glittering chandeliers, colorful booths, jostling crowds, and strange sights.

A man on stilts stalked by carrying a sign that read, WONDER COMICS — BOOTH 319. Balloons and streamers marked vendors' booths. Costumed superheroes mingled with aliens.

"We should take a picture!" said Violet, who had brought her camera. "Stand next to that cardboard cutout of Captain Fantastic."

"What'll we do first?" Benny asked when the picture had been taken.

"Sid asked us to guard his art," Henry

said. "This map says his presentation will be in the Minuteman Room. Let's check it out."

Inside the Minuteman Room, chairs stood in rows. A slide projector waited on a cart in the center aisle. In the front of the room were easels on a stage. A sign tacked to the end easel said, RESERVED FOR AUCTION ART.

"The easels are empty," Jessie noted. "Sid probably has his things locked up."

As the kids turned to leave, they heard a noise.

"What was that?" asked Benny.

"It came from behind the screen," said Jessie.

The kids cautiously approached the stage. Suddenly, the room went black!

But before the lights went out, Violet glimpsed shoes beneath the screen — red shoes with bows on the toes.

Just as suddenly, the lights came back on. Henry stood by the light switches at the back of the room. But whoever had switched off the lights had slipped away under the cover of darkness.

"Did anybody see anything?" he asked.

"I saw a girl's shoes," said Violet. "Red."

"We know it was a girl," said Jessie. "But we don't know why she was here or why she turned out the lights."

"To steal Sid's art?" Benny said.

"Good guess," said Violet. "We'll never find her in this mob, even looking for red shoes."

Henry consulted the map. "Here's Al Conrad's booth. Let's pay him a visit instead."

The ballroom was so jammed, the kids had to wiggle their way through the crowds. At last they reached Al Conrad's booth. Al was talking to someone dressed as Captain Fantastic.

"Do you suppose that's Marvin?" Jessie whispered.

Benny stared at the costumed figure. "I don't know."

"There's *another* Captain Fantastic!" Violet pointed. "And another one over there by that pole!"

"A lot of people are dressed like Captain Fantastic," Henry observed.

Benny stared at the figure leaning over Al's booth. There was something about the costume that wasn't right.

Then he realized what it was. The boots. In the comic, Captain Fantastic wore knee-high shiny black boots. The boots helped him jump over buildings. This person's boots were brown and heavy. Captain Fantastic would never be able to jump over a building in boots like that.

The costumed person left and the kids went over to Al's booth.

"Hello, Mr. Conrad," Henry said. "Remember us? You sold us Captain Fantastic issue number nine last week at the antiques show in Greenfield."

"I remember you," the dealer said. "Isn't this a great show? I hope you're having a good time."

"Yes, it's lots of fun," Henry said, steering Al back to the subject. "You don't happen to have any more number nine comics, do you?"

Al shook his head firmly. "That comic is very hard to find, as you know. I was lucky

to get the one I sold you. I may not see another number nine for months."

Jessie watched the man's face. He didn't
act the least bit nervous. If he was guilty of
selling a counterfeit comic on purpose, he
was certainly playing it cool.

Al looked at his watch. "It's time for Sid
Hoyt's presentation. You don't want to miss
that."

The kids hurried back to the Minuteman
Room. Most of the seats were already taken.

They found chairs in the back near the
control panel, where a red-jacketed hotel
employee was checking switches and cables.
Now red velvet curtains covered the stage.

"There's the Captain Fantastic who was
talking to Al Conrad," said Benny, pointing
to a costumed figure sitting in an aisle seat
a few rows up. "I remember those boots."

Jessie noticed that the person wasn't very
big. It could be a small man like Marvin
Peabody . . . or a woman.

Suddenly Benny blurted, "The house-
builders! That's where I've seen those boots
before!"

"Those *are* construction boots," Henry agreed.

Jessie started to put two and two together.

"There's another Captain Fantastic on the other side of the room," said Violet.

"Irene is sitting next to him," said Henry. "That must be Marvin."

Sid entered the front of the room. Applause broke out. The curtains parted, revealing his original art propped on the easels.

"Welcome," Sid said to the audience. "Thank you for coming. I'll start with some slides showing how I work. Then I'll talk about the art that's displayed up here from issue number nine." He waved toward the easels.

The audience went, "Ahhh."

"And finally, I'll talk about the mistake I made in that comic and reveal my secret signature," said Sid. "The panel with the signature will be auctioned at the end of the day to benefit the Cartoonists Fund."

He gave a nod to the hotel employee who

was stationed by the control panel. The overhead lights dimmed as the projection screen was lowered in front of the easels.

Sid clicked the projector's remote and images appeared on the screen. Sid showed views of his studio, his cats, and his paintings, as he explained each slide.

Suddenly the projector froze. Then all the lights went out.

Someone screamed. Others laughed nervously.

The Aldens were sitting by the door, where a little light from the small window filtered into the room. They saw a shadowy shape near the control panel.

"Who is that?" Benny whispered. "The hotel guy is working on the projector."

The humped shape of the shadowy figure melted into the darkness.

After a minute, the lights came back on. The projector whirred to life again, but the screen was now raised halfway to the ceiling. Sid's slide of his cats was projected onto the easels.

One of the easels stood empty. The kids

knew instantly that Sid's original art panel with his secret signature for issue number nine was missing!

"Both Captain Fantastics are gone!" Jessie reported, scanning the room.

"Quick!" Henry cried. "The thief can't be far! He's got the big panel!"

The children dashed out the back door.

"There's one of the Captain Fantastics!" Benny cried, as a sweep of purple cape disappeared into the crowd.

"Where is the one wearing work boots?" Violet wondered. "He couldn't have that much of a head start."

Jessie drew in a breath. "That person is probably right in front of us!"

"I don't see anyone wearing a costume," said Henry.

"The best disguise is no disguise!" Jessie said. "The person simply took off the costume and is in regular clothes! I know who it is!"

CHAPTER 10

Benny's Super Leap

Jessie raced through the milling crowd to Al Conrad's booth. A woman with blond hair was talking seriously to Al. A flat, newspaper-wrapped bundle was tucked under one arm.

The woman had on stretch pants and heavy boots, just like the boots that one of the Captain Fantastics had been wearing.

Then Jessie noticed a sprinkling of yellow sawdust on the carpet around Al's booth.

"There's the thief," she cried as the others caught up. "She took our note and prowled around Sid's house!"

"And that's Sid's stolen art," Henry declared.

Just then, Sid Hoyt came up behind them and shouted.

The woman whirled. When she saw him, she took off.

But the kids expected this.

"We're the Super-Aldens!" Benny exclaimed, sprinting down the aisle.

The four children ran after the woman, each taking a different route. Being the smallest, Benny was able to dodge in and out among people. He tracked the woman down a long aisle as she made for an exit.

One of the vendors was unloading a new batch of comics. Boxes blocked Benny's path.

But he jumped higher than he'd ever leaped before to dart in front of the woman just as she reached the door.

"Stop right there!" he demanded.

Henry, Jessie, and Violet surrounded the woman so she was unable to escape.

"Who are you?" she asked, breathing hard.

"We're the Super-Aldens!" Benny told her.

"Very funny. Now get out of my way." The woman tried to maneuver around them.

"I'm afraid they can't do that," said Sid, hurrying over.

"Sid!" the woman exclaimed.

"It's been a long time, Dorian," Sid said wearily. "You've got a lot of explaining to do. Let's go back to the conference room."

At that moment, Marvin Peabody and Irene rushed over to them. Marvin had taken off his mask, but still wore the rest of his Captain Fantastic costume.

"What's going on?" he asked. "I just came from Al Conrad's booth. He said he's been robbed. Is that true?"

"He *would* say that!" the woman hissed.

Sid slid the package from under her arm. "I believe this belongs to me. Let's go, Dorian."

Everyone trooped through the exhibit

hall to the Minuteman Conference Room, now empty. They all sat down.

Dorian looked defiantly at Sid. "I suppose you're going to have me arrested, now that you're a famous cartoonist!"

"I want to hear your side first," Sid said. "Kids, this is one of my old friends from ABC Comics. Dorian used to be the inker there, when I was the cleanup man. She quit after my Captain Fantastic comic was published."

"I got tired of making comic books," Dorian said. "So I went into construction."

"We saw you working on the new house near the library," Violet said.

"I saw you, too," said Dorian. "You look like smart kids — the kind who figure things out."

"We figured you stole the note from the library," Henry countered. "And you prowled around Sid's house."

"What gave me away?" Dorian asked.

"Sawdust!" Benny exclaimed.

Dorian looked down. "I guess it's usually on my boots," she said ruefully.

100   *The Comic Book Mystery*

"You were at Al Conrad's booth at the antiques show last weekend," Jessie put in. "You dropped off the fake number nine with the note in it. Al sold it to us by mistake."

"What else did you figure out?" Dorian wanted to know.

Benny spoke up. "You drive the noisy white pickup truck. We saw it where the new house is being built."

"Al told me he'd accidentally sold you the comic before he took the note out," Dorian said. "When I saw you ride by the construction site on your bikes, I followed you to the library, hoping you had the note with you."

"I've been trying to find out who has been passing counterfeit number nines," Sid said. "These kids solved the case. Why don't you tell the whole story, Dorian."

With a heavy sigh, Dorian began. "I was jealous of your success with Captain Fantastic, so I quit. But I kept going to comic conventions. I guess I wanted to get back in the business. I met Al Conrad and we started talking about how hard it was to find Captain Fantastic issue number nine."

Marvin stared at her. "Is that when you got the idea to make fake comics?"

"Yes," Dorian replied. "Al said he could make a lot of money if he had an unlimited supply. He was kidding. But I told him I could copy Sid's style and make a new original. Suddenly, Al was very interested."

"You two couldn't pull this off alone," Sid said. "You still needed to print your copies."

Dorian's eyes flashed. "Les helped me. He's working at Golden Lamp Comics. He secretly had the comic printed."

"Les was my other old friend at ABC Comics," Sid explained to the children. He turned back to Dorian. "I can't believe you thought you'd get away with this scheme."

"We did get away with it," Dorian said, tossing her hair. "At least, until these kids showed up. We had our plan worked out very carefully."

She went on to say that Al would sell the comics only to kids like the Aldens, who wouldn't know the difference between the original number nine and a fake one.

"That's why Al wouldn't let Marvin buy the comic we got from him last week," Jessie interrupted. "He acted like he'd never go back on a deal, no matter how much money Marvin offered him."

Sid nodded. "Al knew a sharp collector would spot the comic as a fake."

Henry spoke up. "But you made a mistake."

Dorian drew in a breath. "Sid's secret signature! I didn't know about it! And I never found it when I copied his drawings."

"How did you find out about it?" asked Benny.

She pointed to Marvin and Irene. "I came to one of the fan club meetings at the library."

Jessie nodded. "We found the business card you gave Marvin."

"I learned about the secret signature at the meeting," Dorian said.

"We're having a contest to see who can find the signature first," Irene put in. "That's why we were so excited about Sid's presentation today. He was going to reveal the location of the signature in number nine. But that was before you stole the art!"

"I had to take it," Dorian said defensively. "Sid's original panel with the signature needed to be destroyed. It was too late for me to go back and make another drawing with the signature in it — Al had already sold a lot of fake comics."

"You prowled around Sid's house last night," Benny accused. "You scared his cats. You were trying to break in."

Dorian slumped in her chair. "But you kids came out. I barely got away."

Benny looked at Marvin. "You followed us from the restaurant the other day. Why?"

Marvin stared at the floor in embarrassment.

"I was jealous," he admitted. "I've been president of the local fan club for three years and Sid had only talked to me at conventions or on the phone. But you kids had just met him and he was taking you out to eat!"

"I appreciate all my fans," Sid told him. "But the Aldens were helping me. No one on the comic book scene knew them, so they could get information that I couldn't."

Violet had a question for Irene. "What were you doing in the conference room? You turned the lights out on us."

"How did you know that was me?" asked Irene.

Violet pointed. "I saw your red shoes under the screen. The other night you had on pink ballet shoes. You like to wear pretty shoes."

"Shoes seem to be giving away a lot of people," Irene said. "I was trying to find Sid's secret signature. I figured I could see it on the original panel and win our club contest. But the art wasn't in there and when you came in — I panicked. I want to win the contest. The winner gets a copy of number nine."

"I've been trying to get a copy for you," Marvin told her. "I know how much you want one. That's why I kept offering to buy the Aldens' copy."

Irene's face lit up with a smile. "That's so sweet of you!" Marvin blushed.

"What are you going to do about me?" Dorian asked.

Sid shook his head. "I'm very upset that my young fans have been cheated. But because you and Les were once my best friends, I won't press charges."

Dorian looked relieved.

"*But* — ," Sid added firmly, "you have to destroy the original plates you made of issue number nine, in my presence. Plus all the copies."

"Don't forget Al Conrad," Henry reminded Sid.

"Don't worry," Sid said. "Al isn't getting off, either. He will call each fan on his mailing list and return their money."

"That seems fair," Dorian said in a small voice. "I'm sorry, Sid. I shouldn't have let jealousy get the better of me."

"I'm sorry, too," Sid said with regret. "We were once such good friends."

Then he went out to the exhibit hall to confront Al Conrad.

"People shouldn't let anything get in the way of friendship," Violet said.

"We'll be friends forever, even if we are family," Jessie agreed.

When Sid came back, he gave a slim package to Henry. "I want to thank you. You kids did a terrific job solving this case."

Henry opened the package. "It's Captain Fantastic issue number nine!"

"A *real* one," Sid said with a grin.

"Thanks!" said Henry, speaking for them all. "Now our collection is complete."

"We have a present for you, too," said Violet. From her backpack, she shyly pulled out a copy of their own comic, *The Super-Aldens*.

"I'll treasure this," Sid said.

With the mystery solved, the kids went back to the exhibit hall to enjoy the rest of the convention.

Benny wondered what their next mystery would be about.

It probably won't be too tough, he thought. *Nothing the Super-Aldens can't handle!*